Deep in the jungle, where only wild things go, Mungo's mum was teaching him what a young monkey needs to know.

"Some things just aren't safe to try alone," she said.

"Why not?" said Mungo crossly. "I'm big enough to do things —

on my own!"

"Now Mungo,"

said Mum, "listen carefully, please.
We're going to go through these
trees. Stay close to me, and hold my
hand. Did you hear what I said?

Do you understand?"

"It's okay, Mum. I won't slip or fall. I can swing across there with no trouble at all," said Mungo. "I'm big enough to do it – on my own!" And off he swung!

And did Mungo hear poor old Snake groan?

No!

Mungo just laughed.
"I told you I could do it
on my own."

"Now, we're going to cross the river using these stones," said Mum. "But, Mungo, I'd rather you didn't do this alone."

"But Mum," said Mungo, and he ran on without stopping, "I'm really good at jumping and hopping. I'm big enough to do it—

on my own!"

And off he sprang!

"That Mungo trampled on my nose!" said Croc.

"Next time, I'll nibble off his toes!"

And did Mungo hear poor old Croc groan?

No! Mungo just smiled. "I told you I could do it on my own."

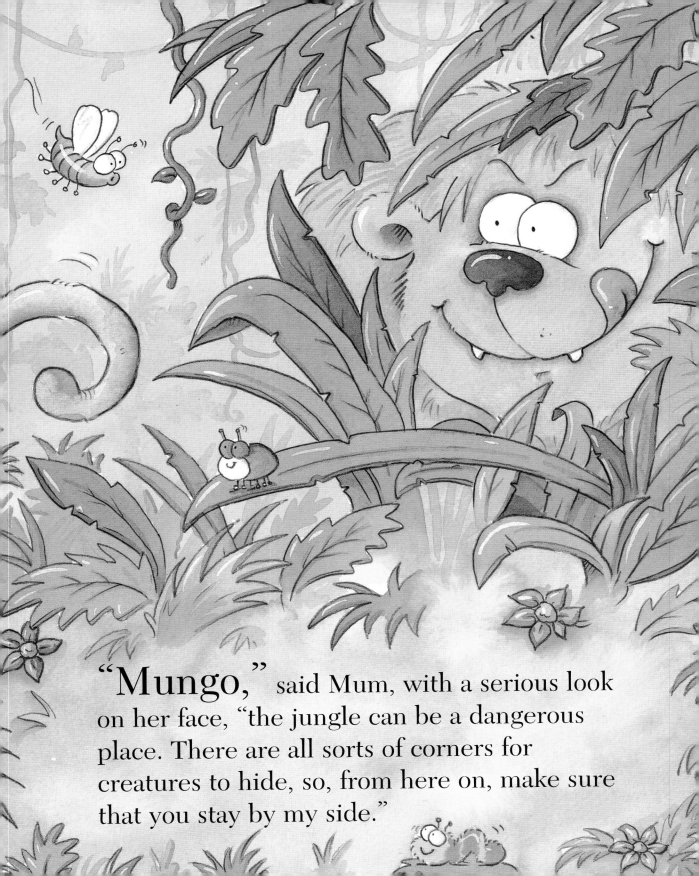

"Mungo," said Mum, with a serious look on her face, "the jungle can be a dangerous place. There are all sorts of corners for creatures to hide, so, from here on, make sure that you stay by my side."

"Oh, Mum," said Mungo, "I don't need to wait for you. I can easily find my own way through. I'm big enough to do it – on my own!"

Lion rubbed the lump on his nose.

"Ouch!

That Mungo's so careless!" he said.

And did Mungo hear poor old Lion groan?
No! Mungo just grinned. "I told you I could do it
on my own."

"I think I've had quite enough for one day,"
Mum said. "So off you go, little monkey!

Now it really is time for bed!"

It was Mungo's turn to let out a gr_oa_n.

"I don't want to go to bed –
on my own!"

"Don't worry," said Mum. "Come on,
kiss me goodnight, and I promise I'll
hold you and cuddle you tight."

Lion roared, "Is that Mungo still awake?" "Yes!" snapped Crocodile.

"Let's help him go to sleep," hissed Snake.

And into the velvety, starry sky drifted the sounds of a jungle lullaby.